Kye-Jeol
계절

Soli S

Ukiyoto Publishing

All global publishing rights are held by

Ukiyoto Publishing

Published in 2022

Content Copyright © Soli S

ISBN 9789360163594

All rights reserved.
No part of this publication may be reproduced, transmitted, or stored in a retrieval system, in any form by any means, electronic, mechanical, photocopying, recording or otherwise, without the prior permission of the publisher.

The moral rights of the author have been asserted.

This is a work of fiction. Names, characters, businesses, places, events, locales, and incidents are either the products of the author's imagination or used in a fictitious manner. Any resemblance to actual persons, living or dead, or actual events is purely coincidental.

This book is sold subject to the condition that it shall not by way of trade or otherwise, be lent, resold, hired out or otherwise circulated, without the publisher's prior consent, in any form of binding or cover other than that in which it is published.

Acknowledgement

Thank you to Zuri and the writers house for your ongoing guidance and support.
To Anku for his passion and dedication.
To Barbie, the little unicorn.
To my family and friends with all my love.
Specially to readers, words cannot express how much your support means to me.

Contents

Winter "Sadness"	1
Autumn "Let's Go"	36
Spring "Motivation"	70
Summer "Love"	109
About the Author	*154*

WINTER "SADNESS"

Scars

Each scar tells a story to be told,
They hide beneath my makeup just to get blowed.
They get darker and darker every day and night;
But see the misery you won't find them in my eye,
I put makeup every morning just to show that I shine,
But inside I am rotten like a dead pet left to be exploit.

Goes

Where ever I go he find me,
He stalks, he haunts me,
Wherever , I go he knows,
He is always their lurking for my ghost.

Sorrow

I don't know how to weep,
I don't know how to sweep,
I am lazy person in love and emotion,
But when the sorrow haunts me,
I weep , sweep my love and emotion under my bed so that it can overrun me in my devotion.

Bae

I loved him with my all heart,
But he took only one second to broke it all apart.
I loved him with all his flaws,
But he took no time to crush it with his super paws.

Judge

He judged me with a single act,
Didn't thought for a one movement
What is correct.
He judged me with a single act,
Shouted like he always do
Just to make me feel regret
He judged me with another act
Separated with me in a second
Like we were never a set.

Handicaped

It's not a physical term,

It's meant for those who's dreams are undone.

Handicap are not born but sometimes are made,

With the worst thought inside their brain

They decompose their body by the poisonous thoughts,

And let them ruin their life by giving them a chance.

Badly

If you love someone badly,
Can u hate the same harshly?
If you love someone truly,
Can u cheat the same intentionally?

Corner

I was made to be raised not to be put in some corner;

I was made to be loved not to be hurt by same lunatic loner,

I lay I die it doesn't matter,

All that matters is I am still alive.

Love Pain

Sometime I think I love the pain,

It's been years, that every month that I feel the shame,

Sometime I think I love the rage,

From my childhood I have been hiding the pain.

I found you, I explain you what I went through every month,

My bleeding Sorrow & now it all make a sense.

Broken Heart

I loved him with my all heart,
But he took one second to broke it all apart.
I loved him with my all flaws,
But he took no time to crush it with his super laws.

Tears

My tears fall like a rainbow drop;
My tear fall like a ranging storm;
They always fall like rain drop,
That's why u can't understand my emotions because they were always there to flaunt.

Time

The time came to me like sweet swift,
The time came to me like a sweet drift,
I don't know what I am fighting for;
But he is really not in love that's all for sure.

Belongings

My heart longs to that men who actually hurts the most,

Who thinks he is perfect without a hoe.

My heart belongs to him who curses and then kisses me every night

Trying to eat me daily like a dead man alive.

Think

Sometime I think did he forget me,
Sometimes I worry did he regret me,
Sometimes I wonder did he loved me,
Sometimes remains for some time.

Twice

I closed my heart not to love again,
I closed myself so only you can come again,
I lied and lied from myself that i can't love you twice;
But love is a funny thing happened often when you don't won't it in.

Stand

I took a stand and stood by it.
I begged and crawled to fall for him.
I saw the love i dreamt in his eyes
But again he took me granted and shattered me thousand times.

Hiccup

There is a hiccup in your words that wanting me to thrive,
There is a pause in our talk that leads us to disguise .
It can be anger , it can be love but more I feel it's the hurt,
When we hit one another with lie, we broke our own heart many times.

Destroy

You create and then destroy,
Remake and then deploy ,
You Rush in my nerve ,

Like world will make you strive.

And crush the things which ever comes in your mind.

You create and then destroy,

Bring me new gifts to enjoy and then next day destroy is with your rage inside.

You create and then destroy ,You create and then destroy.

Work

It's a contest between Work or me,
You say you choose me and then left me ,
Gives it whole day and whole universe.
Point out me for my mood gone worse.
And then say it once again you choose me rest is just work.

It's a contest between Work or me,
Book a night in hotel and then in morning you leave me ,
Alone in the hotel room figuring out some undone
Makes me mad every time but it's just no option.

His Thought

He said , why you have so many mood swings I can't handle it all.
You love , you misbehave and cry a lot.
Sometimes you listen and sometimes you don't ,
Tell me how is this gonna survive for long.
Day and night you're not right , I am not a fool to be blind,
Give me answer or leave me one more time unless we find peace apart for a while.

Doll

Girls are blessed with love and care,
They don't seek your time.
He mistaken me one more time and told me to decide,
I cry ,I fight but for whom he knows the answer and I am right.
He lacks patience and wants me to behave like a doll every time.

Relatable

Silence is all we got on phone,
Nothing more to say,
Nothing more to know
All we do is ,You say? You say?

Why

I know I am strong and brave
Born in ultimate positive family, Saw all the grey's.
I know he hurt me & will do with time,
Why I gave him permission to crush my heart with his eyes.

Someone Else

When I hear he wanted someone else, my heart dropped down,
A stone came above it and smashed it to the ground,
When I heard he wanted my bae, My heart turned into grey,
I put myself in exile and punished myself for loving him divine.

Exile

I exiled myself for becoming who I am,
I treated myself less and didn't cared for a while.
I worked like a slave, dreamed of becoming big
But gained more shame.
I exiled myself for becoming who I am,
I harvested in wrong way and turned myself grey.
I worked like a ant fed my queen with all the things I have to be.

Cheat

Cheat is a small word which resembles with a lie,

Hides the real truth and makes you believe what's not mine,

He cheated me twice, hiding his faults

Once he was awaken and other time he was drowned

He once apologised with heart and he thought I was gone,

No need to make the relation work , let it go to the dawn.

I felt low and low, and asked myself was my love that slow?

Then I felt dark and dark like I was born to handle these scars.

I know nobody is perfect , nobody is alike but all I want is true loyalty ,

Like my god always shine.

He knew how much I love and will forgive him another time.

Because I am too strong to let the past go and nothing hower the coming board.

Killing

Killing is not tough makes a second to do this unjust.

Killing is not for fun, You can either kill a heart or soul for just.

Living is dead serious talk , makes you struggle and bear all the rubbish talk.

No Chance

Seeing him cry makes my heart shrank,
I thought I can forgive him with another chance,
I wanted to love and hug him for the rest of my life,
But how can I forget I had already did this many times.

Dual Combat

Sitting next to him and thinking of you,

Is that a true love which ran out of blue,

Kissing him and feeling for you

Does it make any sense , am I true.

I feel like cheating although I haven't physically touched

But my thoughts had been invaded by the future that is yet to come.

Emptiness

He gave me many lessons on love, life & happiness
He filled me up with kind, peace& no sadness,
On right time I took a walk & left him behind
Never thought he got emptied by giving me the right life.

Bleed

I got burden on my chest but little tenderness in breast.

You got a hole in your soul but nobody to droll,

I got burden on my chest but little hunger to set,

You got a family to feed which makes you to bleed.

Please

He don't know how to love me sober,

He knows how to shout on me,

When he is high he has two face, In which one you don't want to see.

He don't know how to control his emotion and always let it free,

He scream, he shout to make me quite now I am gone as he used to please.

Heart On Fire

Once I said when I will be gone you gonna cry,
Beg for me to come back thousand times,
You'll call me hundred times but no one will lie,
That day will surely come when I will not gonna set my heart on fire.

New You

Now he wears a different ring which shines like gold with diamond on it,

Now he wears a multi colour forgot that he loves only summer,

I can see that he's new , trying to become someone who he barely knew.

AUTUMN "LETS GO"

Drunken Bae

He drinks sometimes,

then love me like a sunflower floating on oceans for a while.

He argues in that time,

as the flower gets drained in oceans by the next ride.

He tried to hit me one time,

as I got drifted back on the beach by the tide of real time.

Dark

Dark ages rise

Dark love dies

One day I will find the light, On that day you will not shine.

Dark ages hide,

Dark love is left behind,

One day I will survive on that day u will cry.

Solitude

I love my solitude,

I love my own time,

I forgot the world what I left behind.

It's gives no pleasure that you are mine as I have left my heart far behind.

I love my solitude,

I love my time,

There is no darkness to be burnt this time.

I found my inner peace just in time,

May be that's what we all need in this busy life.

Cuddle

He wanted cuddles with the morning shine,

But he don't knew I wasn't born to do this time.

He wanted love from my heart to the right,

But he didn't knew that it was destroyed before he come alive.

Demon

She fights with her demon every day,
She avoids the dark to some lay,
We found her strong each day,
But only she knew what's lacking
In her way.

Thought

I thought he will cry,
beg for my love Every time.
I thought he will miss my smile,
Who made him strong every time.
I thought he will come back alive
Like I met him way back when He was 29.

Mother

I can't explain her in some words

Her love is so pure that can't be observed

I don't know how she feels

Every time when I waves off for my dream

She always knew how i felt

Broken, loved or betrayed she sensed.

But still I hesitate to talk about myself ,

Although what she ever do is to take care of me more than herself.

Nails

As they grew we cut them

As they enlarge we shred them

Likewise as love grew we cut ourself

Shutting ourself inside the room so that we can shred them.

Sometimes we let our nails to grow but

Likewise it never ends well even by whatever means we make it glow.

Lipstick

Lipstick either pink or red

It's just meant to be on my lips till the day ends

It motivates the attitude by giving some glint of colour.

Making our life's more soothing by the help of Shea butter

We wore it to look our best but they misunderstood us by these different Colours

Pink for sweetness

Peach for love , red for boldness meant to be sucked.

Hope

I had a hope , who he killed one more time
With his bare hands and eaten me alive
Once I had a hope, now which seems to go
It hurts but I have to let go.

Time

Time made me realise I can be wasted away

It tells me dear you're the yesterday

You have to be strong to fight today odds

Otherwise you will be uprooted from the ground and learn to start it all.

Efforts

Making relation doesn't take effort,

But sustaining a relation needs one.

We fight and fight all the time,

But in the end we cuddle as One.

We try to solve everything by taking a trip of vacay,

But we forget we are not normal so we end up again the same way.

Deep

Our love is deep

I mean real deep,

The world can't understand

We can die together rather than understanding each other.

Confusion

I am standing on two boats
One is high other is low
I am standing on two shores
One is rusty other is mature
My love I am lying between two doors
One is red and other is not shown.

Explanation

I won't say he is bad guy, I won't even lie.

It's just his way to straight and I am still curve in his way.

I won't say he is good guy, I don't even lie.

It's just he is way to caring and possessive sometime.

Busy Life

Rush is all I see in his life,
Battle to settle is all he decide,
Going beyond what the body aches,
He runs for life in every breath he takes.

Cloud Terror

Cloud whispered to sun,
Please don't come today , I like to make an
entrance tonight
Sun shivered and looked terrified,
He sensed the cloud intensions
and ran on opposite side.

Adjustments

When you know he is lying
And cheated you on that day,
What will you do to hurt him in your way?
When you know he is addicted
And cannot stay away,
What will you do to make him away?
Can love be that selfish? Or can love be that blind?
We are not absolute it's not a lie,
No one is perfect I have known that all time,
But I am that fool who always adjust with time.

Lets Go

Let's go to another world, make love and fall for her,

Let's go beyond this point, release yourself to the divine,

Let's go to someplace else, make a new start to fulfil what's it meant.

Chance

I gave him two- three many chance, does he deserve that all,

Being in love or wanted love is that for all,

He cheated, betrayed but not intentional I say,

I was in alcohol making a move on my day,

I was hurt and didn't know until I was sobber,

I left who stood by me in my worse disaster.

I gave him two-three chances, all for my love,

I think there is a god in all of us, Which gives me courage that he can be changed,

If my love will be pure then he will stay.

We can't grantee anyone in this Morden world somehow,

All I can trust Waheguru to make my heart feel sound.

Road Call

I write to make myself calm,

A lot of things has been happen through you have been gone.

I miss you is a simple word to tell you how I feel,

Even we fought on our last day,

But we both know that was a good way to relieve.

Mis Judged

My first and second love made the same mistake,

I gave both options if they want someone other taste,

They denied and I let go.

Feeling myself a little low.

Now I have grown and let it go,

Let the air come in and fill my lungs with positivity of life ,

So that I don't hurt my heart and curse it every time.

Letter's To All

I wrote letters to all , whom i loved or whom not,

I wote my heart out and took a pill to go to new grounds.

It was the love of my family who made me stay longer,

Spent all their wealth and savings to make me feel longer.

Don't Forget

Boys should not forget ,

how hard it was to get her in first place.

Whereas girls should never let go the feeling of getting his attention in first row.

Jealousy

When I am jealous I said it outload,

I said that I am human with my own doubts,

Kindly delete the things I did not want,

Make me proud like a young women with my own flaws.

Dogs On Run

They say men are like dogs beware of us don't fall for the smart,

They play and love like you never had but will be gone in a second as they find another bitch to run.

Open

I am the Entry and Exit of you,
Without me you can't be in.
You can twist or turn with anyone,
But only open by one.

Once

I had love once,
He had me too,
I ran from it,
He caught me too.
It died for me,
But he hold me too
I forget what it meant to be true.

No Hope

Living with him& dreaming of you,
Gives me a break from this untrue,
Wakening with him and thinking of you
Seems like a lifetime with no hope for me too

Shoulder

I have weight on my shoulders of my mother's tear,
I have weight on my feet please give father a treat,
I got courage in my eye to fight or to die,
Now Lazy back summer is hovering to another.

Moved On

My Love, I have moved On,
I do care but now I am done.
My love , I have leaned On,
I think about you when I am alone.
My love, I have Hold On,
Thinking about the possibilities which can be gone.

Present Gift

I know one day everything will come to an end,
We will be left with ourself and no doubt of regret.
I know that day will come ,
So lets forget the past and be present in this one.

Turn

Is it the ending of our relation, Or a new turn God knows what will happen ,When i will know his ultimate reaction.

Is it the ending of our life or a new incarnation,

Loving you is a warm pain with no lots of separation.

SPRING "MOTIVATION"

Fragile

They think that I am a fragile child,
Need to take care by the time.
Assume me with a bird or a fish alive
And eats me every day and every night.
He thinks that I am a fragile child,
can be hurt every time
He Assumed me as a crystal that shines
But baby, I am a diamond who just come alive.

Presence

He comes like a breeze,
blew me up with his little sweet
Smiles like a night scene,
take me to another world where love is all I need.

Miracle

Happens when you believe ,
you haven't shut the door if you want to let it in.
It seems like a normal thing,
But believe me it's all what we need.

Category

There are different types of Girl category,

But non belonged to me.

I was made with steel, Burnt heavily with her bleed.

I was made to be a legend & Fought numerous battle.

I was made to be healed so they put star from the sky so that I can lead.

So how could I can be categorised in some list when I was born with freedom and gave love a gift.

Warmth

I can feel the warmth of her body,
Even though it's been years being separated.
I can feel the touch of her skin,
Even now she never lets me in.
I can feel both sorrow and joy on her face,
Coz m her descendent fallen from the grace.

Women

As a women I have to take many hard decisions many sacrifices;

I have to walk on thorns each and every day just to bring smile on your face.

But what if it's not love

What if it's not a hope because all I was meant to be a Women

Who is the key source of the nature cycle

Who harbour new life's , new hope new dreams into the life.

She is the warm ray of light on your cheek

Which can be felt , seen but can't be touched.

She is the fish in the vast blue sky swims and fly like her choice.

Her heart is the deep ocean, sometimes range like a storm , smashes water from walls to wall

And sometimes silent like a still lake which never ever know how to move without a single rain.

I am a Women meant to give love not to store meant to spread smile not to hold.

I am a Women who's woo makes men proud or who's wooo makes men shout.

Yes I am a women.

Chatter

She chatters when I start wakening up
She chatters till the day is undone.
You can compare her with some bird
But she is always like this from the day she is born.
Clumsy, lovely but little taste of naughty
She is born with all the grace but needs to polish her skills for which god has made.

Relation

Relation is nothing but a understanding term,
Where we trust each other with all of our love
Some days it becomes a nightmare ,
Some days it become a bliss,
But one on another day we are finding our uplift.

Time Again

Time tells me every second you are the one,
It makes me feel like I am not undone
Time tells me every hour that you're not the hore,
It's just the people thought that your odd
Time tells me every day you're not left way
I'll take u to tomorrow where u will be raised.

Fits In

Women always tries to fits in,

Either in their own house or their husbands to let her in,

Either ways they are thrown outside or lured to come back in,

They are always working or just making a living,

Coz Woman tries to fit in -2

Indian Wife

I brought a luck with me,

To shine in another family.

I brought luck in me, to make a new zindgi;

I also brought some faith with me

No matter what happen I will be here to please , & make everything happen.

I Believe

I believe that god is in with me,
In my every action and reaction,
In my every laugh and every tear,
In my every sorrow or confusion,
I believe that god is in my fear-2.

Intutions

Don't know what to say, don't know what to do,

I have a road which is shown and a road where I wanted to ,

I have been prepared to this day will came,

Girl have some patience and it's all be done.

Don't know what to say , don't know what to do,

I am not a coward who will run from you, nor I want to.

I want to make a life, life that I really wanna draw,

But the wisdom inside me keeps saying withdraw, withdraw.

Story Of Love

Love saved me many time
Healed me in seconds from the wars that I fought many times.
Love saved me from becoming devil alive
It's soothes and calm me like I was baby
One time.
Love lasted in me for few times ,
Rest I was sent in dungeon for loving you by my heart this time.

Big One

When do we decide we are mature enough,
Is it the burden of love that comes first.
When we decide we are big enough,
To earn for life or to give it up.
When we decide we are smart enough,
To abandon our parents and cut them up.

I Am

I am ready to be heard, ready to be spoken.
Will tell you my each fuzz and faults ,
My guilt my sour,
Yes I was made to be sugar but I made myself salt.

God

I feel numbness I feel the pain,
It's like I have been slapped a hundred times, Until they said oh it's a mistake.
I have been pulled and dragged with rage,
They said I am a bad omen, burn me at the stake.
Give fire to my body and burn to ashes ,
That will be a greatest pleasure they will take.
They forgot I am a mother, given birth to you all , I can't be forgotten or burn to hell as I am the one who made them all.
They seek revenge and hatred to the one who made them walk,
But the light of truth is far from these blinders,
Coz I am the GOD.

My Advice

I don't need an advise, I know the whole truth,
I have always saw it coming and the two of you.

I don't need an advise just a person to talk,

I know what's right or Wrong.

Your Life

I don't want a physical relation just a loved one,
I don't need to see you naked or want to come in front.
I can imagine how hard your life is,
Spinning as silk wheel , but now thorns are coming out , tearing me to the stream.

Breath To Releave

I breath to release , Exhale the toxin and Take the love in,

I breath to relieve, I forget my past and let the future take me in,

I breath to be alive, Makes my heart pump little high.

Independent

Girls want jewel but I want you, Luxury I can earn

Coz I am not dependant on you.

My parents taught me to be independent, not to be a sloth;

Make your own way child it will help you earn.

You'll fall , you'll get up but most of all you will be running your own sledge.

Old Love

I hope that you read my babies one time

And it will make you feel, how bad some days I felt when you were not in my life.

Your gone for good , it will make you a better man I think that myself sometime.

My friends think I am a stupid girl still thinking of you after 5 years ,

But your memory keep buzzing me every time your near.

Words For X

So far so now, I became a full grown bae,
I got some fat up & cuter what you always said,
Now I take care of myself and eat better than before.
My poems are letter to you even you are far gone.

Manifestation

He is bundle of joy for me,

Sent from above to develop me,

He is the shining light for me,

Always gives me soothing pleasure and glow within the,

He is the manifestation of my desires

Came just on time when I was in trouble.

Years

Years I have spent taking care of my family,
Either its emotional or financially.
Years I have spent praying for love,
When it was in front I don't make it a fuss.
Years I have spent in making mistake
Either I repeat it which is related to my bae.
Years I have spent making the same routine,
Which was not correct and not good for me.

Some Lessons

I knew we met before and will meet again,

Our bonding is undefined,

we feel intentions through sleep sometime.

I knew you know the stress we have this time, You want me more but curse me every night,

No one can understand you like I did,

I loved you in your worst days and in worst sight.

I know these girls love you for your looks,

How masculine now you stood from outside.

I hope you remember the day I motivated to adopt selfcare for real to embrace yourself to become confidant don't appear.

New Commer

I feel myself drowning in deep water, dark dense and see no further,

I feel myself floating in air, nothing to worry

No pain or fear.

I want to be selfish and let me go to another phase,

Guided by the true soul which is making my heavens way.

But my mother love is so bright that she will bring me back from dead and make my heart once again run for new commer.

To All Mothers

Though I let her down in front of many,

I loved her a lot and make her my pray.

I want to give her all what she can't relate ,

Making me a new women and creating my identity to this world.

I hope you always stay till I am alive.

I don't want to see you can go while I am breathing fine.

Papa

He is so calm, so lovable I can't get angry on him,

Even when he is not available within.

He don't buzz me and don't say a little bit.

His shadow is so strong , his aura daily grows to my kin,

I don't like to see him old, makes me feel what I can do

To make him young all along.

Connections

All I can recall that we have good and bad,
I am too emotional and my love is all that I have.
I am not a professional nor too talented,
I just started my learning without any connections.

Living Dream

Time has been very harsh on him,
As he left his childhood to become something.
Time has been kind to him ,
Now he is a successful man living his every dream.

Women

I saw her working every day, I don't know why she prays,

I saw her lying unconscious on the ground when she's too tired to make any sound,

I saw her hiding in between the darks so that she can be the women of other hearts.

Unicorn

I saw a magical unicorn,
Unicorn by my side
He made me glow every day,
While work through the night.

I saw a magical unicorn,
His hairs has golden shine,
Lashes were falling heavy,
While the thorn burns bright.

I saw a magical unicorn,
Whose body is strong an long.
He walks on water in middle December,
Making me hard to tumble.

Dreams

I am a big dreamer and want to be a achiever,

Have a big house and lots of money to be spent out.

I am a big dreamer and wants to run the house,

Having little kinds and wondering lifes way to feel proud.

Succeed

I want you to succeed , see you there where we dreamed,

Babe I want to be free, I can't be in your arm and let you go there thee.

Seasons Gone

It's been two days since we parted, looks like some seasons have gone,

I wished I could write you a letter,

Letter of our love, Of our parted ways,

So that we remember each other with no mistakes.

So that we can still love in our new ways,

So that we can still hope that tomorrow will be a better day.

Lift Up

I feel no stone on my chest,

Just my drowning heart with no regrets,

Now am in this new arms and I feel free,

Ready to take off And sky is beneath me.

I feel no pain in my heart,

Just the moist on our skin is left.

We hug we cuddle we do this all the time,

but see we don't get bored as we are running out of time.

SUMMER "LOVE"

Hear

I like to hear my heartbeat when he is around,

I get nervous when he is stares me in that dumb sound.

I lurk for his attention that shouldn't be happen,

Coz all I knew he is sent from above and made to create miracles.

Steps

Baby steps he take,
Sometimes jumps a little late.
I need a normal walk,
So that side by side we can talk.

Imagine

What if we never met,
I would have been living a normal life.
I wonder the roller coaster will never start,
Until you set my world on fire tonight.

Unexplained

My eyes are out , brain is shut;
He took the juice, And left me to thirst.
My eyes are out, my mouth is shut,
He say don't speak the truth,
Otherwise you will be judged.
My eyes are out, now my hands tremble,
I wanted to stop but now my heart is undone.

Strange Eye

I look at you , you look at me,
Like we have known each other.
You saw me I saw you too,
Like we have loved each other.
Now that we really know,
I wish that we have stayed together
Because stranger seems stranger either we know each other.

Black Eyes

His deep dense eye finds me everywhere,
Like a golden swan finds his golden mate.
His deep sense eye looks into my eye,
Like a rainbow sky wants to just shine.
His deep dense eye scans me every night,
Like a thunderstorm ranging behind my smile.

Empty Bed

It craves me to call him

Even I knew he is far away

The emptiness resides in me

As he always slips away

I try to hide but my eye can't

He knew I know but still the empty bed remains attached.

One Love

We always desire but we never do,
One love is neither passionate not true;
One love can be achieved by hurting others;
One love is nothing but a true wisdom.

Night Out

Night out, I thought that it will work out
Night out, on that day we hardly doubt
Night out ,we stay but at the end we surely engage
Night out, I should have shout
Night out, it's a worse play out.

Red

Red bench with red light,

Makes my heart pump up this time.

Green grass Purple flowers this time,

Bring me the spring tomorrow night.

Yellow light where it shines?

Is it the aura of my love which lighten the mood every time.

Stranger

Your nice stranger ,
You should stay away from me ,
I am a collateral damage,
Ready to be free.

Reach

Your Reaching heigh for the sky,
I'm reaching low to the snow.
We make the line in between the sky , Put rainbows
to blow.

Truth

There is love beyond sex ,
And sex beyond Love.

Mark

Mark my word I have met you before ,
Mark my words I have loved you for sure,
This time I don't know how to behave
But I wanna have your single taste.
Can't you see, you're meant for me
But now you're crying for someone else to be.

Winter Love

Winter night seems cold and rough,
Good for cuddles if you got a loved one,
Harder for single how to spend this time,
Temperature is too cold for me to make outside.

One More Time

I can feel his breathing on mine
Hot with mint flavour like he knew we goanna kiss
this time.
He tried to grab my hand and hold it for some time,
A shooting star falls at our feet and I zinked one
more time.
He took me by his arms and dances in garden like a
new wedded bride ,
Everyone was watching what a stupid boy and girl are
having fun one more time.

Sail

He sails 4 months and gives the rest to mine,

He works few weeks and loves me every day and night

Don't call him sailor as he is an explorer,

Who less sail and discover more the bodily pleasure of mine.

Oni's Bundle

He is bundle of joy for me,
Sent from above to develop me,
He is the shining light for me,
Always gives me soothing pleasure and glow within the,
He is the manifestation of my desires
Came just on time when I was in trouble.

Little Fantasy

It seems like a fantasy, I never thought I can love you.
And now it seems we were meant to do.
He comes to pick me and we go on a drive,
He like to eat a lot and then cuddle for a while,
We talk hours and hours until the days fall off,
Now we get worried as to start our story for long.

All In One

His hands are strong , when he grabs me its tight as a claw.

His eyes are slow show, let you dream the world in one row.

His Back is so smooth that it will make you feel, you're not so cool.

But best is always left behind, his smile who kills people with arrows strike.

Surprise

One day he came and bring flowers alive,

Said " darling it was meant to be in your arms this time".

One day he came and got two tickets to fly,

He said we need vacation badly coz I love you with all my heart my life.

Pleasure

He gave me first and nothing else,

Gave me pleasure to call him Love and forget the rest.

He makes me feel like more than a family,

I know I am riding a roller coaster where nothing is set free.

Lost

Because of him I left so much, Didn't have a choice to make all forget.

Because of him I lost so much, no friends no family but just two of us.

It's the cost of love we have to pay,

But only if we are loyal to each other every day.

I Magical Journey

A magical journey all began, like some movie he sweeps me within,

He know all the tactics which makes me fall every time,

We just started a new love which makes us want each other every time,

We bath, we eat at same time,

We run, we cook to keep ourself excite.

Breakfast in bed he gives me every time, either its morning or a date night.

Glitter

Glitter nails I see some females,

Grey hair, I see his mare,

Glossy lips , he wants me to kiss,

Straight hairs are no more but a perfect clear shit to wear.

Gold ring I am waiting for him,

Tired days are no longer my ways.

Nasty

Empty Trees Please bring the summer sneeze,

Birdie call no more a stroll,

Sunlight shine looks like a rainbow in my eyes,

Fat day will keep you busy if you want to wear bikini and betray.

Young Love

One is called soulmate , One is called twin flame.

Difference I don't see much but I know what I had,

You were all that I had a true one.

You heard me crying a lot , made my saddest day undone,

Listen me every night talking till 4 am cursing you for not letting me sleep,

even when I am the one.

One is called soulmate & one is call twin flame

I had both but I let go, I will tell my babies about a young love

Made me glow.

Innocent Dream

I remembered when I was teen you took me under the bridge and made a love scene,

You tore my dress of white and pink,

I was shy how to ride bike and hide what we did,

We took pictures and memories what i think.

Now all I have is a blurry thought of these years when we were something.

Next Time

I pray my love grown with every time;

I wish we grew old holding hand and smiling for another life.

I know we had a little time but in next birth we will surely be fine.

Summer Haze

His glittering eyes and glittering lies,
I fall for it once and while,
His curly hair and curly shade,
I want to smell it with the summer haze.

Own Timing

I am late in everything, but it's not the end,
I am a starter in this new phase a new chapter begain.

Different Lane

Day shines like his smile, goes into dawn like he hides,

I know he misses me every time when I call his name,

We know we are made for each other every single day,

Our body is separated by this living order strange,

But one day we will united in the different lane.

Delight

He comes and go in my dreams,

Touches my body with his flirting rings,

I haven't seen him just felt,

Breaths me out when he left,

I call him screaming every time but don't know his name

As he is my delight.

Psyco

I can love you multiple times,

I can cry love and laugh at the same time.

People thing I am weird or some kind of psycho

But that's the sign of true person loving you at a time.

Teenage Dream

I am living a teenage dream,
Wearing his shirts and waking up next to him.
He see through my eyes and says he love me.
His eyes gets wet when he meant to be.
I am living a teenage dream,
He is still sleeping and I am writing these
To tell the whole world what he meant to me.
I am living a teenage dream.

Out Of Time

Giving myself break and I fall for you,
Sometimes I regret what I did too.
I have watched him grow and now letting him go.
I know we have a special place for each other we knew.
Giving myself break and moving on with you,
Sometimes I think why I did that too.
I should be single and let the karma decide,
But I can't help my feelings running out of time.

Little Fun

Sex is a powerful thing, One can seduce and other will fall for it,

Not having a single thought what is supposed to be done,

Is it a trap of Tv or just the flow of fun.

Falling

Falling for him is like falling from the tree,

So smooth so slow but so relieved,

Falling for him is like falling from the night,

Softly getting drifted away with the wild wind to touch the sky.

Falling for him is like falling from the height,

Hairs floating and want to do this one more time.

Sexy Guy

When he drinks, he is the most sexy guy,

Makes your heart skip a beat every time.

When he dances with wine, makes you forget who you are dressed this time,

When he kisses you in his arm he makes your day worth to wait.

Dark Desires

He ties my arms & legs with the bed sometime,

Makes me feel naked and then the goosebumps arrive,

I feel so embarrassed of my body having little hairs this time,

I should have known he will come and shaved it on time.

Rubbing

I can hear my heavy heart which makes my hands go numb,

but I can't control them or make it stop for a while.

I can hear his heavy breath too, which gives my body a push,

To jump on him like to ride.

I stretch his arms and kiss his whole body with mine

And that how a winter days go like rubbing each other every night.

Eternal Gift

He has given the best gift in my life,

The gift of Writing.

He observed it in and broke me down to let me shine this

New Chapter

Starting a new chapter, new life is like a giving birth to yourself with no one's hard work this time.

Self Love

I learnt a lesson in short time , took me 5 years to realise,

Self-love is the Ultimate love of all time,

Don't give your 100 percent to another life.

Love yourself and be kind,

Then only someone will love seeing true heart in your life.

About the Author

SOLI

Soli is an artist, poet and writing enthusiast. Her work swings between the whimsical and woeful, expressing a complexity beneath its childlike facade. She is also a trained classical dancer and has great fondness for romantic novels and paintings. Her first book was a self help book which raised the social issues that we usually face in our day to day life.

Follow her on Instagram & Twitter @*authorsoli*

www.ingramcontent.com/pod-product-compliance
Lightning Source LLC
LaVergne TN
LVHW041949070526
838199LV00051BA/2963